Mother Earth

For all children, big and small, who belong to Mother Earth.

"Poets warned us, writing of the "heartbreaking beauty that will remain when there is no heart to break for it." But what if it is worse than that? What if it's the heartbroken children who remain in a world without beauty? How will they find solace in a world without wild music? How will they thrive without green hills edged with oaks? How will they forgive us for letting frog-song slip away? When my granddaughter looks back at me, I will be on my knees, begging her to say I did all I could.

I didn't do all I could have done.

It isn't enough to love a child and wish her well. It isn't enough to open my heart to a bird-graced morning. Can I claim to love a morning if I don't protect what creates its beauty? Can I claim to love a child if I don't use all the power of my beating heart to preserve a world that nourishes children's joy? Loving is not a kind of la-de-da.

Loving is a sacred trust. To love is to affirm the absolute worth of what you love and to pledge your life to its thriving—to protect it fiercely and faithfully, for all time."

-Kathleen Dean Moore, from "The Call to Forgiveness at the End of the Day"

Helani Claire likes to catch ladybugs and pick other people's flowers. She lives in a small green bungalow with her mom and big brother that lacks flowers but is filled with love.

Earth laughs in flowers. -Ralph Waldo Emerson

Helani's mom is a bit odd. She doesn't drive a car or use a cell phone. All the other mommy's wear pretty dresses and high heels. Helani's mom prefers to be barefoot and throws on whatever she grabs first, whether it matches or not! When Helani gives her outfit a skeptical eye, she rolls her head back and laughs hysterically. Helani looks at her crazy attire and starts giggling too.

THINGS TO BELIEVE IN

trees, in general; oaks, especially;
burr oaks that survive fire, in particular;
and the generosity of apples

seeds, all of them: carrots like dust,
winged maple, doubled beet,
peach kernel; the inevitability of change

frogsong in spring; cattle
lowing on the farm across the hill;
the melodies of sad old songs

comfort of savory soup;
sweet iced fruit; the aroma of yeast;
a friend's voice; hard work

seasons; bedrock; lilacs;
moonshadows under the ash grove;
something breaking through

-Patricia Monaghan

Helani wants to get manicures and go shopping at the mall to buy new clothes. But her mom doesn't like those things.
And Helani can't understand why.

She is a breath of power, a pure vision of glory,
A reflection of eternal light, a spotless mirror of goodness.
She is one, but she can do all things.
She remains herself, but renews all things.
Each generation she creates prophets and holy ones,
For she is more beautiful than the sun and the stars,
Mightier than the earth itself, and she orders all things well.

Wisdom 7:25-8:1

She says they poison her, they poison the people who make them and they poison the Earth.

"If we destroy the Earth, we destroy ourselves." -Chief Jackie Thomas

Helani walks everywhere with her family. Along the way, they stop to pet every-single-dog they see. Much to the annoyance of her brother, Helani lingers to smell each flower, making wishes on dandelions whenever she can. "Why don't more people walk places instead of drive?" Helani asks. "I think cars should go extinct, *not* polar bears."

"Can anyone believe it is possible to lay down such a barrage of poison on the surface of the earth without making it unfit for all life?..man is a part of nature, and his war against nature is inevitably a war against himself." -Rachel Carson, *Silent Spring*

One day, Helani and her mom were home sick.
They were both *seriously* grumpy.

"Sing
Because this is a food
Our starving world
Needs.
Laugh
Because that is the purest
Sound.
 Because that is the purest
Sound."

- Hafiz

Helani's mom went to lie in bed. She was happy to finally rest.

I roam
sacred ground

my body is my altar
my temple.

I cast a circle
with my breath
I touch the earth
with my fingers
I answer
to the fire of my spirit.

My blood
pulses in time
with larger rhythms
past, present, future
connected
rooted
breathing.

The reach of my fingers
my ritual
the song of my blood
my blessing
my electric mind
my offering.

Breathing deep
stretching out
opening wide.

My body is my altar
my body is my temple
my living presence on this earth
my prayer.

Thank you.

-Molly Remer, Body Prayer

Helani started shouting at her from the other room. "Come here right now! I need you."

The sage lives in harmony with all
below heaven.
She sees everything as her own self;
She loves everyone as her own child.
All people are drawn to her.
She behaves like a little child.

-The Tao Te Ching, 49th Verse, Revised

Helani's mom was tired. She did not like to be yelled at. "I will come when you stop shouting," she snapped back.

"Power is not brute force and money; power is in your spirit. Power is in your soul. It is what your ancestors, your old people gave you. Power is in the earth; it is in your relationship to the earth." -Winona LaDuke

Helani felt more and more angry. Her voice kept getting louder, and louder and louder.
Her mom stayed in bed, feeling more and more exhausted.

Give us this day our daily bread, and let us eat, remembering. Instead, our female children starve themselves bone-thin to repudiate your flesh, we slice it out of our bodies, we hide it in our fat, we choke ourselves and vomit, re-enact that first shame under the Tree, when making a human form, the labour it entails and the blood that comes with each moon became a curse.

Oh let me rekindle that fierce mother love— and weep for the mother slayers. Can I shield my daughter from the truth that she is powerful and because of that she may be killed? This is your secret, the power of birth and the real miracle of blood turning into milk (not water into wine). We, who rely on these first stories to understand our place in the world, have had a bone stuck in our throats or should I say, an apple core, for a long time.

Give me back my mother love, my rising star, my Venus, the sun's circle of life: let the man in the sky stop building missiles and fighter F14 jets for South Korea, Iran, Pakistan, Israel and South Africa, let the Old Man in the US Senate hear the voices of the women. Let the African governments hear the voices of their raped and damaged daughters. Let the Lebanese women rise, let the Pakistani women rise, let the Afghan women, the Chechen women, the Colombian women, the Rwandan women, the Palestinian women, the Venezuelan women, the Chinese women, the Uzbekistani women, let the women in the veil, the women in purdah, the women stoned to death, the women doused with kerosene for their dowry, the women thrown down wells for honour, the women sliced open and sewn shut, the women interred, let all the women remember you. Your light was not always this dim.

-Jenn Boire, Mother-famine

"You are supposed to be my mom. You are supposed to help me. You are supposed to take care of me. You don't care about me at all!" Helani cried.

The earth is my sister;
I love her daily grace,
her silent daring,
and how loved I am
how we admire this strength in each
other,
all that we have lost
all that we have lived
all that we know:
we are stunned by this beauty,
and I do not forget;
what she is to me,
what I am to her.

-Susan Griffin

Helani's mom looked down, searching for an answer.
"I always take care of you. And I always love you. But, sometimes, you don't treat me that nice."

"Until you want for another what you want for yourself you have not truly believed."

-Prophet Mohammad (PBUH)

Helani looked down, feeling a little sad. Her mom felt pained just watching her. She realized that sometimes she did not treat her mother that nice, either. She expected her mom to be and do everything for her,

"And since women carry within the cellular structure of their bodies the imprint of all creation, they carry the consciousness not only of their own suffering but also the suffering of the earth: the wounds and desecration caused by a patriarchal culture who sees God only in heaven. The pain many women feel in the core of their being is also the unacknowledged pain of the earth cut off by this masculine way of thinking from the divine- exploited, damaged, and desecrated by our patriarchal culture. This suffering too needs to be accepted and sanctified, so that the energy of life can flow freely within the earth. The earth has cried and women have heard its cry, felt its tears."   -Llewellyn Vaughn-Lee

They both began to cry.

"If we could strip away the ideologies that separate us, stop the greedy destruction, and meet by the riverside, we would discover that we are all children of the same earth and that our lives are patterned by the ceremonial flow of the sun, moon, seasons, and tides. We are all one in the spirit and in the body."
-Sedonia Cahill and Joshua Halpern

Her mother straightened up to tell her a story.

"We have to rewrite the world."   -Ursula K. Le Guin

"In the beginning, there was the first Mother. She was round and full and plentiful..." Helani's mom spread her arms out around herself to show the fullness of Mother Earth.

We have a beautiful
mother
Her green lap
immense
Her brown embrace
eternal
Her blue body
everything we know.

-Alice Walker

Helani's eyes widened as her mother continued. "She gave birth to all that we see around us: the birds, the sky, the oceans, the kitty cats.... She created everything and she took care of all of it. She worked and she worked and she worked. She was happy to do it. She loved all of her creation."

Like a caring mother
holding and guarding the life
of her only child,
so with a boundless heart
of lovingkindness,
hold yourself and all beings
as your beloved children.

-Buddha

But after thousands of years with no rest, She became tired. Her husband sat on the couch and rested—and then took all the credit for Her work. Her children threw their dirty garbage around for her to pick up, unaware of all She was doing to keep the world afloat. They forgot about Her needs and took Her for granted.

"Without community, there is no liberation."   -Audre Lorde

Over time, Mother Earth became sick. She could not stop coughing. She could not get out of bed. Her children kept demanding Her attention, but She was too ill to help them.

"Only if we understand can we care. Only if we care will we help. Only if we help shall all be saved."
-Jane Goodall

Finally, some of her daughters began to notice Her absence. They began to deeply miss their mother, but they could not find Her. They looked inside their televisions but She was not there. They tapped frantically on their video games, but She could not reside in a small plastic box. They searched the entire mall but She wasn't there, either.

"The forest teaches us union and compassion.

The forest also teaches us enoughness: as a principle of equity, how to enjoy the gifts of nature without exploitation and accumulation. Tagore quotes from the ancient texts written in the forest: "Know all that moves in this moving world as enveloped by God; and find enjoyment through renunciation, not through greed of possession." No species in a forest appropriates the share of another species. Every species sustains itself in cooperation with others.

The end of consumerism and accumulation is the beginning of the joy of living."   -Dr. Vandana Shiva

None of those things made them feel any better. They became lost and started to cry.

"Most of us these days find ourselves less than fully well, physically or mentally – somehow out of balance. We can feel our dis-ease, but don't ordinarily know the solutions to it. If we knew how to make ourselves well, we would almost certainly do so. The great gift of the Goddess is such a healing. To the individual, she brings personal well-being and an experience of fully living. To humanity, she could bring the harmony that comes with a recognition that we are all connected in spirit to this planet. We depend upon it for survival and we owe it the gift of life. "   -Vicki Noble

When they stopped all their searching and were still for a while, they remembered some of the lullabies She used to sing to them.

You are the One within me,
star-bright in midnight dark,
who echoes in the ocean
and dances with the lark,
who smiles in the mirror moon
and on the tide of dreams,
rocks me soft and gentle
to the songs of
mountain streams.

You brought me into being,
breathed life into my soul,
you birthed me to my body,
you knit me as a whole,
my mother, you embraced me,
your kiss upon my brow
sighed your spirit through me
and it fills me now.

I feel your spirit fill me,
you call from every star,
in whispers from within me,
in echoes from afar,
you pull upon my
moonstruck mind,
you open out my soul
and like an unfurled sail, it fills
and I am whole.

-Ruth Calder Murphy,
Hymn to the Goddess

Our Mother is the forgotten parts of ourselves, they realized.
When we hurt our Mother, we are hurting ourselves.
And when we hurt ourselves, we also hurt Her.

"In exploring and celebrating the ancient ways, we affirm our commitment to healing the planet and each other, since we see the earth as the body of our sacred Mother, we are much less likely to wound and damage her. And if we honor our own ability to know, to be wise and powerful – if, in fact, we celebrate our own Goddess-essence, we heal the split so many of us have sustained between our daily, conscious selves and our inner, deep selves." -Cait Johnson & Maura D. Shaw

They began to help their Mother clean up the mess that had been made. They taught their brothers how to help them. Slowly, Mother Earth became better and more vibrant.

" The Earth is your Mother and Grandmother. When you walk on the Earth, you are making a prayer to her." -Burleigh Mutén

They came to her and knelt at her bed. "Mother, we have missed you," they told her. She smiled. "I have missed you too my darlings. And I love you more than you can imagine."

"They're the asherah trees of the Bible...The first temples dedicated to Goddess. There were thousands of them in ancient times. She says women are planting them again, along with other sacred trees of Asherah... palms, olive, apple, cypress...it took a few thousand years to make people forget her; it will take time to help them remember." -Amy Logan, The Seven Perfumes of Sacrifice

"But I am still very tired," she continued. "I need you to look within yourselves, remember everything I have taught you and help me so that I can heal."

"Breathing in, I cherish myself. Breathing out, I cherish everyone else."

The Dalai Lama requests that everyone recite/chant this 5 minutes a day.

"Your video games and electronics are hurting me, and they are hurting other children too. Nearly everything for sale in the malls is poisoning my streams and soil. Someone has to make all these things, and it is often poor children in other parts of the world, working in very bad conditions with toxins that no one should touch."

"Unless we return to an understanding that nature is our first religion and the visible world the altar of worship, we will not be able to make the necessary sacrifices to heal our dying planet." -Andrew Gurevich

"That is the reason that you always need more and that you don't stay happy. When you hurt other people, you hurt me. And when you hurt me, you feel it within yourself."

"A society that could heal the dismembered world would recognize the inherent value of each person and of the plant, animal and elemental life that makes up the earth's living body; it would offer real protection, encourage free expression, and reestablish an ecological balance to be biologically and economically sustainable. Its underlying metaphor would be mystery, the sense of wonder at all that is beyond us and around us, at the forces that sustain our lives and the intricate complexity and beauty of their dance."   -Starhawk

"So, take a deep, deep breath. Find that spot in the center of your being where all your power resides. Hold in your breath as long as you can. Repeat this until you feel really, really strong. "

Breathe. Feel the air enter your lungs. Breathe. Feel millions of oxygen atoms permeating your lung membranes, entering your bloodstream, being delivered to every cell in your body, fueling the fire of life within you. Mother is feeding you. She feeds you and sustains your life with every breath.

Let your consciousness move now down to your feet. Keep going down through the floor, to the ground. Penetrate the ground with your consciousness as though you were growing roots into the Earth. Deeper and deeper. Sense her massiveness. Her ever-abidingness.

Feel her hold you to her. Gravity is her embrace. Feel her love. Allow her love to flow into you, up through the soles of your feet, through your legs and torso to your heart, your shoulders, your head. Bathe in her love. Breathe.

Let her love permeate every cell. Let your heart fill with her love. Let it swell with love, from her, for her.

She nurtures you in every way.
The air you breathe is her.
The food you eat is her.

Let your love and gratitude grow. Let it flow out to her, to Father Sun, and to all your brothers and sisters of the plant and animal kingdom.

We are all mother's children, beloved by her, nurtured and protected from the harsh reality of outer space.

-Julia Scofield Russell

"Then, pick something –one thing—that you can do yourself, or with your sisters and brothers, to help me clean up. Maybe it is watching less TV. Perhaps it is buying used clothes—or making your own. Maybe it is helping your mom and dad with the recycling or planting a garden. But whatever it is, do it until you are really good at it – and then add something else."

"I am only one, but still I am one. I cannot do everything, but still I can do something; and because I cannot do everything, I will not refuse to do something that I can do." - Helen Keller

"After a while, you will see your brothers and sisters are helping too. And then, I will arise from my rest and join you."

"We need Goddess consciousness to reveal earth's holiness. Divine feminine imagery opens up the notion that the earth is the body of the Divine, and when that happens, the Divine cannot be contained solely in a book, church, dogma, liturgy, theological system, or transcendent spirituality. The earth is no longer a mere backdrop until we get to heaven, something secondary and expendable. Mater becomes inspirited; it breathes divinity. Earth comes alive and sacred. And we find ourselves alive in the midst of her and forever altered."   -Sue Monk Kidd

Helani's mom closed her eyes. The tears were gone. She had found her center again. She looked up and saw that her daughter was looking at her. "I'm sorry," she said.

What if our religion was each other
If our practice was our life
If prayer, our words
What if the temple was the Earth
If forests were our church
If holy water--the rivers, lakes, and ocean
What if meditation was our relationships
If the teacher was life
If wisdom was self-knowledge
If love was the center of our being.

-Ganga White

"I'm sorry too," Helani replied. They snuggled in together and sang a song for Mother Earth.

The Mother Goddess takes manifests multitudinously as earth, water, snake, owl, toad, bear, flower, fruit.
She has but doesn't possess, acts but doesn't expect.
She who is Earth and Her people are the same.
We mend and weave the web of Life together.
May the Great Mother continue blessing us all and calling us back to Life.

-Adapted from Sacred Resonance

They began to hear the birds singing outside their window.
As they looked out, they saw beautiful trees rising to the sky, and flowers blossoming all over their backyard.
Children were running into the center and dancing in a circle.
They were singing and laughing. They had come back to Mother Earth. And She embraced them all.

"The time has come, the walrus said. Perhaps things will get worse and then better. Perhaps there's a small God up in heaven readying herself for us. Another world is not only possible, she's on her way. Maybe many of us won't be here to greet her, but on a quiet day, if I listen very carefully, I can hear her breathing."

-Arundhati Roy

A Covenant for Honouring Children

"We find these joys to be self evident: That all children are created whole, endowed with innate intelligence, with dignity and wonder, worthy of respect. The embodiment of life, liberty and happiness, children are original blessings, here to learn their own song. Every girl and boy is entitled to love, to dream and belong to a loving "village." And to pursue a life of purpose.

We affirm our duty to nourish and nurture the young, to honour their caring ideals as the heart of being human. To recognize the early years as the foundation of life, and to cherish the contribution of young children to human evolution.

We commit ourselves to peaceful ways and vow to keep from harm or neglect these, our most vulnerable citizens. As guardians of their prosperity we honour the bountiful Earth whose diversity sustains us. Thus we pledge our love for generations to come."

-Raffi Cavoukian

Trista's Acknowledgements

This book is written with my deep hope for a better world for my children and stepchildren: **Helani, Joey, Ferdinand and Carl-Richard**. I love you all very much.

Helani and **Joey** also helped with (brutal) edits.

In addition, I'd like to thank the following people:

My husband **Anders** is the most supportive and encouraging man I have ever met. Anders helped tremendously with both books and the Girl God website. I love you sweet.

My mother, **Pat Kendall**, for her never-ending generosity and love.

My dear friend **Tanya Lamb** has been there through thick and thin since we were girls. I love you Lep!

Alyscia Cunningham for her continual support and sisterhood.

Ruth Calder Murphy has been a tremendous source of encouragement and inspiration to me.

Lastly, it has been an honor to work with **Elisabeth** and her husband **Morten** again. There is no end to how much I admire Elisabeth's talent and how grateful I am to both of them for their contributions to this book.

Elisabeth's Acknowledgements

To **Trista**, kindred spirit and inspiration, for her wonderful drive and vision, patience, and faith; for her love and devotion to my art and for choosing me to participate in her magnificent and important book.

To **Morten,** my beloved husband, handyman, driver and computer wizard. You are my source of inspiration, advice and love, for all the work and time put into the book, and in my artistic work in general.

To **Anders, Pat, Arika**, and all the skillful and dedicated helpers out who saw the importance of this book. Thank you all so very much.

To my friends and family, for believing in me and backing me up to believe in myself as an artist.

Kristin and **Marianne**, for being best friends as well as sisters and faithful audience at most of my exhibits.

My mother, **Ingeborg**, who has passed along her warmth, care, and universal love. Always by my side.

My father, **Olav**, who introduced me to drawing and visual art, saw the talent in me, backed me up in choosing the path of arts, and encouraged me to learn more and seek knowledge.

Last but not least, to **Helani**, and all children, for asking those wonderful questions that make us look deeper into existence.

Love and kisses
Elisabeth

Quotations

Whenever possible, we obtained both the permission and the blessing of the author. It is with gratitude and appreciation of these beautiful words that we quote them in our *Mother Earth book.*

In order of appearance:

Kathleen Dean Moore www.riverwalking.com
Excerpt from "The Call to Forgiveness at the End of the Day" from the book *Moral Ground: Ethical Action for a Planet in Peril* shared with permission of the author & publisher: Trinity University Press, www.tupress.org

Patricia Monaghan www.patricia-monaghan.com
"Things to Believe In" *Grace of Ancient Land*, shared with permission of the author's husband, Michael Mc-Dermott, & publisher Voices from the American Land www.voicesfromtheamericanland.org.

Molly Remer www.goddesspriestess.com
"Body Prayer" shared with permission of the author.

Winona LaDuke www.honorearth.org
Quote shared with permission of the author.

Jenn Boire http://www.jenniferboire.com
"Mother-famine", excerpt shared with permission of the author.

Susan Griffin www.susangriffin.com
Excerpt from *Woman and Nature: The Roaring Inside Her*, published by Sierra Club Books, shared with permission of the author.

Llewellyn Vaughn-Lee www.workingwithoneness.org
Quote shared with permission of the author.

Ursula K. Le Guin www.ursulakleguin.com
Excerpt from "The Fisherman's Daughter" from *Dancing at the Edge of the World*, copyright 1989 by Ursula K. Le Guin. shared with permission of Grove/Atlantic, Inc. Any third party use of this material, outside of this publication, is prohibited.

Alice Walker www.alicewalkersgarden.com
"We have a Beautiful Mother" from Her Blue Body Everything We Know: Earthling Poems 1965-1990 Complete by Alice Walker. Copyright 1991, 1984, 1983, 1981, 1980, 1979, 1977, 1975, 1973, 1972, 1970, 1968 by Alice Walker and renewed 2003, 2001, 2000, 1998, 1996 by Alice Walker. Reprinted by permission of Houghton Mifflin Harcourt Publishing Company. All rights reserved.

Jane Goodall, PhD, DBE - Founder, the Jane Goodall Institute & UN Messenger of Peace www.janegoodall.org www.rootsandshoots.org Quote used with permission of the Jane Goodall Institute.

Dr. Vandana Shiva
Excerpt from "Everything I Need to Know I Learned in the Forest", Yes! Magazine, December 2012. Shared with permission of the author.

Vicki Noble www.motherpeace.com
Excerpt from *Motherpeace: A Way to the Goddess Through Myth, Art, and Tarot*, shared with permission of the author.

Ruth Calder Murphy www.ruthcaldermurphy.com
"Hymn to the Goddess" shared with permission of the author.

Cait Johnson www.caitjohnson.com & Maura D. Shaw www.maurashaw.com
Excerpt from *Celebrating the Great Mother*, shared with permission of the authors.

Burleigh Mutén www.burleighmuten.com
Quote from The Lady of Ten Thousand Names: Goddess Stories from Many Cultures. Published by Barefoot Books. Copyright 2001 by Burleigh Mutén. Shared with permission of the author.

Amy Logan www.amylogan.com
Excerpt from *The Seven Perfumes of Sacrifice*, shared with permission of the author.

Andrew Gurevich
Excerpt from "Forgotten Wisdom of the Chauvet Cave: The Sacred Feminine and the (Re)birth of Culture.", Popular Archaeology, shared with permission of the author.

Starhawk www.starhawk.org
Excerpt from *Truth or Dare: Encounters with Power, Authority, and Mystery*, published by HarperOne, shared with permission of the author.

Sue Monk Kidd www.suemonkkidd.com
Excerpt from *The Dance of the Dissident Daughter: A Woman's Journey from Christian Tradition to the Sacred Feminine*, shared with permission of the author.

Ganga White www.whitelotus.org
"What ifs" from Yoga Beyond Belief: Insights to Awaken and Deepen Your Practice by Ganga White, published by North Atlantic Books, copyright © 2007 by Ganga White. Reprinted by permission of publisher.

Arundhati Roy
Passage from her 2002 speech, "Come September" shared with permission of the author.

Raffi Cavoukian www.childhonouring.org
"A Covenant for Honouring Children"©1999, 2010 Centre for Child Honouring shared with permission of the author and the Centre for Child Honouring.

Praise for The Girl God

"This book is a must for our daughters" -Christy Turlington

"...a remarkable addition to interfaith literature for children and especially for young girls."
-North American Interfaith Network

"Want to change the world in one generation? Every parent should read and share The Girl God with their children... and with their hurting inner child. It is full of stunning artistic illustrations by artist Elisabeth Slettnes. Both have collaborated in this extraordinary gift to humanity. A true masterpiece!" -Vrinda Puja

"...one of the most beautiful children's books we've seen..." -Every Mother Counts

"The Girl God: a picture book to show girls that god can be a girl, god is inside, god is an idea, a positive action or good deed, god is open to creative interpretation and should be about everyone. A great book to dispel the myth that god is male with wonderful illustrations by Elisabeth Slettnes. Empowerment for our girl children." - A Girl's Guide to Taking Over the World

"This book will be one I treasure, for it is rare indeed—the articulation of the divine feminine for both children and adults, a bridge between our spiritual beginning and our spiritual future, a spark for the reawakening of humanity." -Elizabeth Hall Magill

"A deceptively simple story about a whimsical young girl named Helani Claire, who would make Emily Dickinson smile as she deconstructs the patriarchal god of her father with the bluntness of a child. Akin to: If Kate Chopin was still alive, writing (and self-publishing) children's books. Elisabeth Slettnes' colorful paintings are feasts for the spirit, as are the addition of selected quotes and poems. Wisdom abounds."
-Philadelphia Weekly

8442608R00023

Made in the USA
San Bernardino, CA
10 February 2014